CRASH WAGON
Book One - Family Ties

By

Jason Eric Pryor

Prologue

2499 A.D.
New Year's Eve
Earth

This was not the life Brett wanted. Not for him or Jordan. It was the kind of life that would get him and his sister killed sooner rather than later. He was betting on sooner, given the current situation they found themselves in.

The streets on this side of Laguerto were dangerous enough without members of The Monarchy showing up. What did they want? Why were members of a rival crime family encroaching on their turf? They probably thought they could move through the crowded streets of the New Year's Eve celebrations unnoticed.

He'd noticed them, however. And now he and Jordan had them cornered in a vacant alley. Perfect place for bad things to happen. He didn't care why they'd come, as long as they didn't stir up any trouble.

"You boys are about a day's flight from Portozuela, aren't you?" he said. "Pretty far from home."

One of the five interlopers stepped forward. "Last I checked, it wasn't against the law to travel outside of your home city."

"I guess that depends on which law you're talking about. By Central Government standards, sure. You can come and go as you please. But people like us - we live by a set of laws that's a bit less liberal. Wouldn't you agree?"

"Trust me," the man said. "I'm here on business."

"What kind of business?"

"The kind where I plant enough lead in you to make you radiation proof and show you off like a trophy to my boss."

"Really? That's your plan?" Brett said. "You figure you'll just show up with a few other head cases, take me down so you can get a pat on the back by your family head?"

Some of the men turned their attention to Jordan. From the corner of his eye, he could see why. She had slowly moved her hand to the pistol that was strung low on her hip. The two of them were outnumbered. He couldn't let this get out of hand. Knowing Jordan, she would start the fight quicker than the Monarchy thugs.

"Why don't we all just calm down, okay?"

"Tell that to your sister, Hawkins. Looks like she might be feeling a bit heroic."

Brett shot Jordan a look. Not now. Look for your moment. She glanced at him, moved her hand away from her gun, and turned her focus back on the men.

"There. She's fine. See? No need for lead to fly."

"That's up to you," the man said. "My boss may be even more impressed if I was to show up with you alive. Won't be a need for shooting if you were to come along with us quietly."

"Well, that's not an option," Brett said. "Not really looking to be someone's prisoner. Especially yours. Plus, it's New Year's Eve, and I'd kinda like to stick around here. I hear they're shooting off fireworks later on."

"Doesn't look like you're leaving me much choice," the man said.

"I've got a notion, and correct me if I'm wrong, but I'm thinking your boss doesn't even know you're here," Brett said.

"It's called taking the initiative," the man said.

"It's called stirring up a hornet's nest. You Monarchy boys have Portozuela. My old man's got Laguerto. It's been relatively quiet between the two families for a while now. Why don't we try to keep it that way? At least for another year."

"Great things happen to risk-takers, Hawkins," the man said. "Personally, I think it's time to start mixing things up a little. It's starting to get boring. I say we start the new year off with a bang."

Brett was getting a bad feeling about how things might turn out. This guy was not the kind of man you could reason with. He had learned on several occasions that it's nearly impossible to talk someone out of a fight once their mind is set on starting one. An intelligent man can use reason and logic as an initial option. When intelligence is absent from a man, he's controlled by savage ferocity.

"Something tells me you aren't just wanting to make me a trophy to impress your boss," Brett said. "Sounds like you got a little bloodlust looking to come out."

The man looked at Jordan. "Maybe it's just the regular kind of lust." He took a couple steps toward her.

"Hang on a minute," Brett said, stepping in front of her. "This is between you and me. You can leave her out of it."

"You know," the man said. "Maybe you're right. Maybe I do want more than just a trophy."

"Well, you don't want this. I can assure you." Brett said. "How long do you think it will be before some of our men see you and yours? They won't be as chatty as I've been. My guess is you've been spotted already."

The man took a couple more steps toward Jordan. "That's what I brought my boys for."

"I'm not going to tell you again. Stay away from her."

The man drew and aimed at him, catching Brett off guard. Why did I talk so much?

Two shots rang out, but it wasn't Brett that took them.

She found her moment.

Chapter 1

Nine years later

The *Graffiti* was in a slow spin, drifting aimlessly through space. All navigation systems were down, as well as life support. Most of the crew had been killed in the initial explosion, including the captain, so Robert Price, the *Graffiti*'s pilot, had taken over as the highest ranking crew member.

Graffiti was a transport ship, traveling from Mars with a shipment of minerals, and was only a few days away from reaching the Earth city of Port Frisco. Luckily, it wasn't in deep space - the area of nothingness that stretched between Earth and Mars, dotted only by three space stations along the way, *Sapphire Station, Emerald*

Station, and *Ruby Station*. Since they were only a few days from breaking Earth's atmosphere, Price had hope their signal would be picked up by someone. Anyone.

Unfortunately, the explosion in the *Graffiti*'s engine room was leading to a core meltdown. The temperature in the ship continued to rise. The engine room doors had been sealed to slow down the rising radiation levels and several survivors were frantically adjusting controls outside of it to attempt to lower the temperature in the core.

It wasn't working.

The remaining survivors huddled on the *Graffiti*'s bridge, where the radiation levels were at their lowest. Price could hear their muted voices as he monitored the scanners, desperate for help to appear. He transmitted another request for aid.

"Repeat. This is transport ship *Graffiti*. We are heavily damaged and approaching core meltdown. We have taken many casualties, including our captain. We are requesting aid from any ship that may pick up this signal."

Price waited for an audible reply through the ship's communication system. Thank heavens it was still operational. He scanned the darkness outside through the *Graffiti*'s front viewport, hoping to see a sign that someone had heard him. All he saw were the stars, rotating in an unfamiliar pattern due to the uncontrollable roll the ship was in.

Another explosion shook the *Graffiti*, escalating the muffled concern on the bridge to excited shrieks. Price keyed a command into his console which ran a scan of the ship. An updated damage report lit the main monitor. The cargo deck had lost pressurization. At least he had the foresight to move everyone to a safe place.

He leaned forward, accessing the controls to transfer another request for aid. Before he could press the button, however, he heard a faint break in the static. He froze and raised a finger to silence the survivors' chatter. The bridge fell completely silent. Then, the comm speakers crackled to life.

"Transport ship *Graffiti*. This is Captain Joseph Shaw of the rescue ship *Crash Wagon*. We are en route to assist you. Stand by."

Whoops and cheers broke out behind him. Price fell back into his chair and wiped the sweat from his brow with the back of his sleeve. They weren't out of the woods yet, but their chances had gotten a lot more favorable.

* * *

Jaimie Ellis sat at the helm of the *Crash Wagon*. Her ship had left *Sapphire Station*, the last deep space station before reaching Earth, and was on its way to King's Bay to refuel and restock when she heard the *Graffiti*'s distress call. She always had two distinct feelings when she picked up a call for help. One was of genuine concern for the people that needed their aid. The other was a sense of relief that she had been able to pick up their signal. Space was big. Even if you stuck to the trade routes between Earth and Mars, being in distress could mean days, or even weeks before anyone heard you. Some people just didn't have that long. She was happy when they finally got within communications range and Shaw was able to let *Graffiti* know that help was on the way.

The lights of the main console reflected in the lenses of her black-rimmed glasses. She wore her sandals to the bridge, but they now sat on the deck beside her chair. She wore a loose-fitting pair of cargo pants and sat with one leg folded under her. Her shirt was old, but loved, the faded words, 'Port of Orleans Flight School' barely visible across its front. Her black hair was pulled into a loose and disheveled pony tail.

Captain Shaw stood behind her. She'd alerted him that they were coming within range of the *Graffiti*. He looked through the *Crash Wagon*'s front viewport, arms folded across his chest. He was still in what could be considered good health for a fifty-nine year old man. Jaimie considered it a privilege to work on his ship. There was a certain fatherly quality that she saw in him. He seemed to view his crew as family, and she had no problem with that. It was how it should be.

Her thoughts became focused on the job as the *Graffiti* came into view. "She's in a spin."

"Activate the RAID," Shaw said.

Jaimie spun her chair to the left, and accessed the RAID console. The words, 'Remote Access Integration Device' lit up on the home screen. She brought up the scanners and locked on to the *Graffiti*'s signature. Within seconds, she was able to view the *Graffiti*'s systems as if she were sitting at its helm.

"I'm in," she said.

"How's she look?"

"All major systems are down, including navigation."

"Let's steady that spin she's in."

"I'm on it."

She straightened her glasses and accessed the navigation panel on the RAID console. The *Graffiti*'s thrusters were highlighted on the screen. Jaimie tapped them with her finger. The thrusters, which were unusable to the *Graffiti*'s pilot, roared to life under her control and she was able to stop the ship's spin.

"That's better."

"What's the radiation level?"

Jaimie slid her finger across several more screens on the console until she came to the one that allowed her to access their safety sensors. She scanned *Graffiti* for radiation.

"Higher than it should be, but not dangerous yet. It's concentrated aft."

"Get me a layout of the ship."

As she accessed the schematics, Shaw raised the

comm's mic to his mouth to speak to the *Graffiti*'s pilot. Jaimie found it interesting that with all the advances in engine, construction, and terraforming technology, the comm system was still basically a glorified radio. It was a way to communicate with other ships using their own comm system. This was not the same as the earpiece communicators that the individual members of the *Crash Wagon* crew wore. The earpiece communicators were on a private network, used so that all six members of the crew could speak to one another and be aware of what was going on during rescue operations. They could also be tracked, which allowed her to know where everyone was at all times. This had proved to be helpful on several occasions.

"Transport ship *Graffiti*. This is rescue ship *Crash Wagon*. Do you copy?" Shaw asked.

"We copy," the pilot replied. "Standing by."

Relief flooded her when she heard the pilot's voice. More often than she cared to think about they arrived too late to save the victims. She never blamed herself. She knew she always did her very best to reach them in time. But, it still didn't make it any easier to handle those situations.

"Good," Shaw said. "Here's the situation. I'm sending my people over to assist you. I need you, and everyone else on board, to do as they tell you. If, at any point, I think my people are in danger, if they are attacked, threatened, disobeyed, or looked at funny, they will fall back to the ship. We will then disengage our boarding hatch, put you back in that spin you were in, and go about our merry way. Do we have an understanding?"

"Yes, Captain," the pilot said. "We're grateful for the assistance."

"Okay," Shaw said. "Stand by and prepare for docking."

* * *

Brett Hawkins and the boarding team made it to the *Crash Wagon*'s boarding hatch. Brett wore light body armor and carried a handgun. He was the first mate and Captain Shaw's right hand. He was used to command the boarding team. Today, that team consisted of himself, his younger sister, Jordan Hawkins, and the *Crash Wagon*'s mechanic, James Foster.

Jordan also wore armor. She, however, carried an assault rifle. She had her favorite handgun slung low on her hip, as well. Boarding an unfamiliar ship had inherent dangers. An ambush could be waiting. The RAID could be used to shut down a ship's weapon systems, but it was up to Jordan to put an end to any human threats once they were onboard. Brett trusted her to do her job. She was very good at it. Even before joining the *Crash Wagon* crew, he had always been able to count on her.

Foster carried a pistol and wore a backpack

containing his tools and other small mechanical devices. The pistol was for his own protection. His main concern was the condition of the damaged ship. If he could fix it, at least enough to get it safely to the closest repair station, it would save them the trip of dropping the survivors off at a port. Even if they were heading to a port city anyway, caring for survivors meant spending precious resources. Plus, fixing a ship meant a nice cash bonus from the Guild.

"We're in place, Captain," Brett said, using his earpiece communicator.

"Jaimie's sending you the ship's layout now," Shaw said.

The trio checked the screens located on the small gauntlets they each wore. They were given the *Graffiti*'s layout, as well as radiation and temperature readings.

"Okay," Brett said. "This is a standard board and rescue situation. Jordan will lead, followed by me, then Foster. Jordan and I will get the survivors aboard the *Wagon*. Foster, you head to the *Graffiti*'s core regulator. See if you can't do what you mechanics do. Maybe keep it from exploding and killing us all."

"Sounds good," Foster said. "I just have one question."

"What's that?"

"Why does Jordan always go in first?"

"Well. I don't know if you've noticed or not, but she carries a really big gun."

"I hope I'm not interrupting anything," Shaw's voice said in their earpieces. "But we're about to dock with a ship that has an overheating core. So, can we wrap this up? Or do you two need a little more time to discuss the 'Jordan's gun size' issue?"

"Nope," Brett said. "I think we're good."

"Fantastic. I know I feel better," Shaw said. "Now, let's help these people."

The *Crash Wagon*'s gangway extended to the *Graffiti*'s boarding hatch. It locked on and created the airtight seal needed to maintain pressurization.

"Okay, guys. You're good to go," Jaimie said.

"Copy that," Brett said. "Okay. We're about forty-five feet away from a lot of heat, panic, and unpleasantness. If something bad happens to us, we won't be much good to these people. Keep your head in the game and stay sharp. Let's move out."

Jordan led the trio through the gangway to the *Graffiti*'s docking hatch. She opened it and a wave of heat swept across them. She held up her hand, attempting to shield her face while still keeping an eye out for any potential threats. They were met by the pilot. He held his hands up to show he wasn't armed.

"No one is carrying a weapon," he said.

The trio stepped into the ship. It was hot. Really hot. Intermittent streams of sparks shot from crevices in the bulkheads and bounced on the deck below. The acrid smell of burning wires filled the air.

"Where are the survivors?" Brett asked.

"All but three are on the bridge. The others are attempting to slow the core's heating," the pilot said.

Brett turned to face Foster. "You head down there and see what you can do to help them. Jordan and I will assist the others to the *Wagon*."

"I'm on it," Foster said.

Brett watched him disappear down the corridor through a wall of haze. He turned to face Jordan and the pilot. "Okay. Let's get to the bridge."

* * *

Foster approached the sealed doors of the engine room. The three men in front of them turned to look at him, their faces stark with fear and anxiety. They were drenched in sweat. Foster could feel the excessive heat through the metal doors.

"I'm here to give you a hand," he said. "What have you tried?"

The men didn't question him, or where he came from. "There's an emergency nitrogen cooling system in place," one said. "But it didn't activate. We're trying to get it online."

"Jaimie. What's the RAID telling you about an emergency nitrogen cooling system?" Foster asked.

"Stand by," Jaime responded.

"Can I get that double time? We're kind of in a hurry

here."

"She said stand by," Shaw said.

Foster made a mental note regarding his earpiece communicator. Try not to forget that everyone on the *Crash Wagon*'s private network can hear what you say.

"Sorry, Captain. It's just really tense in here."

"Keep your focus, Foster."

"I've tapped into the cooling system. I should be able to activate it and stop the meltdown from here," Jaimie said.

"Great," Foster said. He turned his attention to the three men. "Okay. I need you to head back to the docking hatch. There's two more from my ship assisting the others there now. In case something goes wrong, I need you all to be off this ship."

"What are you going to do?" one of the men asked.

"I'm gonna monitor the cooling system. Make sure we're good. Maybe we can save your ship. Now go!"

The three men ran towards the docking hatch as instructed.

Foster shrugged off his backpack and took a small device out of it. He connected some of the wires to the panels on the wall. The device gave him the temperature and radiation readings from inside the engine room. The temperature was dropping.

"Foster," Shaw said. "What are you doing? Your communicator shows that you haven't left the area yet."

"Just tapping into that core data, Captain. I've

confirmed the temperature is dropping." He turned the dials on the device.

"Jaimie said she can take it from here," Shaw said.

Jamie's frantic voice broke into their conversation. "Wait a second, something isn't right. The cooling system is failing! It's heating back up!"

"Get back to the ship, Foster!" Shaw said. "That's an order!"

Another explosion rocked the *Graffiti* and Foster was thrown to the deck. He felt sparks and heat wash over his body.

"Everyone check in!" Shaw said.

"I'm okay," Foster said. "Just a little rattled." He began to disconnect his equipment and pack it back into his backpack.

"Jordan and I are fine. We're sending the last few survivors through the gangway," Brett said. "Doc's gonna have injured."

"The explosion knocked the cooling system completely out. The core's heating up again. I can't do anything about it," Jaimie said.

"Everybody catch that?" Shaw asked.

"Got it," Foster said. "I'm heading to the docking hatch now."

Fires were spreading throughout the ship as he headed down the corridor. He could almost feel the temperature rising. Smoke filled the air and it was getting harder to breath.

A large explosion shook the *Graffiti* and slammed him into the handrails. Part of the deck above broke free and crashed into the corridor. Foster fell to the floor, his leg pinned under the debris, and a sharp pain shot through his left knee. From the feel of things he might have cracked some ribs as well.

"I've got a problem here!" he said.

"What is it?" Brett asked.

"That last jolt pinned me down. I can't free my leg."

"Where are you?"

"One of the catwalks leading from the engine room."

"Brett. According to his communicator, he's roughly one hundred-seventy feet aft of the docking hatch," Jaimie said.

"Jordan," Brett said. "Get the last of these people on the ship. I'm going after him."

"Okay, people! Let's move!" Jordan said.

Foster struggled to free his leg but failed. Footsteps reverberated through the metal deck and Brett stepped through a cloud of smoke and sparks.

"How bad is it?" he asked.

"My knee is twisted. Possibly cracked some ribs. Also, I fell on my gun."

Brett squatted down to try to lift the corner of the deck that had Foster's leg pinned. He couldn't budge it.

"Did you really think that was going to work?" Foster asked.

"I'm sorry. Am I the one that's currently pinned under

a burning piece of spaceship? Shut up while I figure out how to get you out of here."

Brett grabbed a piece of the handrail that had broken free. He jammed it under the corner of the decking, forming a makeshift lever.

"Okay. I'm gonna lift the corner of this deck up as much as I can. Try and pull yourself free."

"I suppose it's better than plan A."

Brett pushed the piece of handrail up. It began to bend under pressure, but the corner of the deck seemed to shift a little.

Foster tried to slide his leg out. It hurt like the devil and he clenched his teeth as he forced his muscles to work.

"This ain't a bag of feathers here!" Brett said.

"Do not drop that, Hawkins!" Foster concentrated, forcing his knee to bend. It throbbed violently, and he was afraid he would lose his lunch from the pain, but finally he managed to wrench his leg free.

Brett dropped the deck back down with a crash. The entire corridor shook from the impact.

"It's getting pretty inhospitable in here," he said as he helped Foster to his feet. "Can you walk?"

"Think I'm gonna need a little support." Foster wasn't sure if he could put any pressure on his left leg.

"Guys!" Jaimie said. "Can we move it along? That core is really heating up!"

"Just be ready to get us out of here once we're

aboard."

Ramming his shoulder under Foster's arm, Brett half-carried, half-shoved Foster to the *Graffiti*'s docking hatch. They climbed in and made their way the forty-five feet to the other side. The air cooled as they got closer to the *Crash Wagon*'s open hatch. After climbing through, Brett sealed it and disengaged the gangway. The indicator panel went from red to green.

"All clear, Jaimie! Get us out of here!"

The *Crash Wagon* turned to port and the thrusters engaged. It wasn't the smoothest of departures, but they were in a hurry. As they pulled away, the *Graffiti* began to break apart. Several smaller explosions billowed through its hull before one final blast engulfed the ship in flames. All that was left of it were chunks and fragments floating through space.

Jaimie exhaled after guiding the *Crash Wagon* to a safe distance. Shaw stood behind her.

"Brett. Jordan. After you get Foster and the others to the infirmary, meet me in the galley," he said. He removed his communicator. "Well. That was closer than I would've liked."

"We've had closer," Jaimie said.

"No, we haven't."

"I know. I was just trying to calm myself down."

Shaw patted her on the shoulder. "You did good, little lady. Set a course for Earth and come to the galley to grab a bite."

Chapter 2

Brett sat in a chair at the end of an old wooden table. The galley was the one place on the ship that didn't feel like a ship. It was much warmer in tone for one thing. He liked spending time here. Jordan, Shaw, and the *Graffiti*'s pilot were with him. Jordan sat on the counter, drinking a bottle of water. She had removed the upper half of her light armor suit and was wearing a simple tank top with a picture of a gun on it. Brett figured she always wanted a gun on her, even if it was just a drawing. His sister was a woman, no doubt, but he felt sorry for any man that might question her toughness.

Captain Shaw was a good man. A fair man. He was sure he had seen a lot. He had a very solid rescue record.

Brett hadn't worked for many captains, but he felt comfortable thinking that Shaw was one of the best. He watched as the man greeted the *Graffiti*'s pilot.

"I'm Captain Joseph Shaw. Welcome to the *Crash Wagon*."

"Thank you, Captain," the pilot said. "Name's Robert Price."

"Mr. Price," Shaw said. "I truly am sorry for what happened to your crew and ship. You have our condolences."

"That's much appreciated, Captain. We're all grateful for what you and your crew did. You saved our lives. It's unfortunate that I have to bring this up, but everything we had that we could've paid you with went up with our ship."

"You pay taxes to the Central Government, Mr. Price?" Shaw asked.

"Of course."

"Then you've already paid us. Taxes are what keeps us in business. Just like the military or police agencies."

"Then it's a tax I happily pay."

Brett wondered how many people were happy to pay the Rescue & Assistance tax. He figured the number was probably on the low side. At least until they needed aid, like Mr. Price and the *Graffiti* survivors. He also wondered how much profit the Rescue & Assistance Guild made. It had to be astronomical. It wasn't like they had a lot of expenses. The Guild got all that money from the government to pay the rescue ship crews that were spread among Earth, Mars, and every little moon and space station in between. But that was it. Every rescue ship captain independently owned his or her own ship. So, the Guild didn't have to spring for them. Every crew had to provide their own fuel and supplies, so the Guild was free and clear there. They had a pretty good racket going.

"Mr. Price," Shaw said. "Where were you heading?"

"Port Frisco. We thought the ship could handle the last leg of the trip. In hindsight, we probably should've stayed on *Sapphire Station* long enough to double-check the engines."

"I'm sure under normal conditions you would've been just fine," Shaw said. "But, with Earth and Mars being on opposite sides of the sun right now, the trip is a lot harder on the older engines. Most stay on *Emerald Station* until the travel lane to *Sapphire Station* is a little more favorable. I'm surprised you made it as far as you did."

"Staying on *Emerald Station* would've been a wise choice," Price said. "I would like to see more of what it has to offer. As many times as I've been there, I've still never seen all of it. Sapphire is much smaller and more crowded. Once we got there, we made the decision to try to make it the rest of the way to Earth."

"Well, I was thinking of heading to King's Bay to refuel and replenish our inventory. But Port Frisco isn't much farther. We'll get you there."

"I appreciate that, Captain. Will there be anything else? I'd like to return to the infirmary to check on the survivors."

"Of course," Shaw said.

Price got up from the table and walked toward the corridor. He stopped and turned to face Shaw. "Captain? If you don't mind me asking, how did you control our ship?"

Shaw smiled. "Let's just say your tax money had something to do with that, too."

"Very well," Price said. "Whatever it is, you're putting it to good use." He turned and left the galley.

That reminded Brett of one big expense the Guild had that he had forgotten about. The RAID. It was an amazing piece of technology. It granted control of any ship within its range to the rescue ship. Even if the ship being rescued had damaged systems, as long as they had power, they could be accessed and controlled remotely using the RAID. One particular good use was being able to shut down a ship's weapon systems for the protection of the rescue crew. It was a very expensive piece of equipment, and one that the Guild was required by law to provide for all rescue ships that were licensed with them. The only other vessels that could have a RAID legally installed were law enforcement vessels.

But, other than that, it was still a pretty good racket.

"Why are we going to Port Frisco?" Jordan asked.

"You got somewhere else you need to be?" Shaw asked.

"I just didn't think we were a shuttle service."

"Would you rather us launch them out of the airlock? I mean, I realize I may not be the smartest captain around, but I'm pretty sure rescuing people and then launching them into space defeats the purpose of a rescue vessel. Wouldn't you think?"

"We were heading to King's Bay to refuel and restock. I assumed our plans would stay the same. They can find transport to wherever they need to go from there," Jordan said.

"Port Frisco is only the next port over. We can get what we need there, and get these people to where they were going. It's your classic two birds scenario," Shaw said.

Brett loved his sister. But she had one of those personalities that could clash with, well, anyone. He figured he better step in before she dug herself into a hole. Like she usually did.

Jordan slid off the counter. "Going there is a waste of resources! We shouldn't-"

"Jordan," Brett interrupted. "We're gonna need an accurate inventory so we know what to pick up when we get to Port Frisco. Why don't you go get on that." He gave her a hard look. "Now."

Jordan returned Brett's look, then turned and walked out of the galley.

"Let me ask you something, Brett. Has she always been so ornery?" Shaw asked.

"Ever since we were kids."

"Huh. I bet that was fun for you."

"She'll be fine. Just let her huff and puff a while. Taking inventory will give her something else to focus on."

"I'll have to remember that. In the meantime, I need you to put together a report and have Jaimie send it to the Guild. I'll get a head count from the doc of the survivors we rescued."

"Okay."

"Oh, and make sure the report mentions we were first on the scene as well as the only ones on the scene. They tried telling me last time that 'only one on the scene' implies 'first one on the scene', but that's not true. They are two separate bonuses. I looked it up. So, don't let them give you the run around. We need all the cash bonuses we can get."

Brett smiled. It was true. If you let them, the Guild would weasel out of paying you what they owed you. You had to stay on your toes when dealing with them. Quite a racket.

"I'll get on it," he said.

* * *

"Hey, Doc?"

Doctor Donovan Barrett turned to see where the call had come from. The infirmary was his space. He knew every nook and cranny of it. He had an organizational system that some would say bordered on chaos. But he always knew where his things were. For example, he had a coffee mug half full of room temperature coffee sitting on his desk from that morning. He would have to remember to make himself a fresh brew in his coffee pot, which was currently located...well...not important.

Donovan had not shaved in several days, which was normal. He was known as much for displaying a three-day beard, as he was for his unkempt hair. He enjoyed fine clothes, but he didn't enjoy taking care of them. His trousers, which were frayed at the ankles, and his shirt, which needed ironing, were both very expensive when purchased new. Donovan preferred them a little worn out. He felt it made his wardrobe look more personal.

He walked past several beds that were occupied by *Graffiti* survivors until he came to the one currently occupied by Mr. James Foster.

"You called, Mr. Foster?"

"How's my knee look?"

"It's sprained, but it will be fine. I would advise you to get plenty of rest, and refrain from allowing large portions of spacecraft to fall on it again."

"Good advice."

"Indeed. But then again, I am a doctor."

"You have any idea where we're going next?"

Donovan placed his hand on his chin and allowed his eyes to drift in thought.

"Well. I have several ideas, actually. We could be continuing as planned, which would be King's Bay if I'm not mistaken. Of course, King's Bay is really a dreadful place this time of season. It would be almost cruel to drop these poor people off there. They've been through enough hardship at this point, what with their transport exploding. We could be en route to Port Frisco. It's only slightly out of the way and a much better place for them to find another transport. Although, the best port on this side of the continent is Diego City. I can't say I would mind going there. Beautiful city. Another thought I have, and this is a long shot, is that we may not even be going to an Earth city. If these people are settlers, we may be heading to Mars. As you are probably aware, Mars contains many cities and settlements that would be a likely destination for—"

"Maybe I should rephrase my question," Foster interrupted. "Do you know where we're going?"

Donovan paused to think. "No."

Shaw entered the infirmary. "How's he doing?" He made his way to Foster's bed.

"Captain. I didn't even hear you come in," Donovan said.

"Yeah. I'm like a cat. How's his knee?"

"Sprained. But, as I was just explaining to Mr. Foster, he will be fine. I estimate he'll be up and about in two to three days' time."

"I was just asking the doc if he knew where we were going," Foster said.

"Port Frisco," Shaw said.

"Ah! My second guess!" Donovan said. "But, to be honest, I'm just thankful we aren't going to Mars. I'm not very fond of that planet."

"Really?" Shaw asked. "I would've never guessed. Last time we were there you were so much fun to be around."

"In my defense, I was under the weather."

"In my defense, I didn't leave you there."

Donovan enjoyed the captain's quick wit and sense of humor. It was commendable for a widower to maintain that aspect of his personality. It had been over fifteen years since Captain Shaw's wife died. And every year, without fail, the captain remembered her through photos and videos on their anniversary. Donovan had often thought about how nice it must be to think back on your wife with such fondness. He knew that if his ex-wife died, he would probably be celebrating that day year after year.

"I think we both know you would be bored without me as part of your crew," Donovan said.

"You'd be a tough one to replace, Doc. That's for sure."

"Well, I hope that's not gonna be the case with me," Foster said.

"What's on your mind, son?" Shaw asked.

"I have to leave, Captain."

"Leave? Why?"

"Another opportunity has presented itself. You know how it is."

"Are we really that bad, Mr. Foster?" Donovan asked. "You've only been with us a few months."

"You're a fine bunch. It's just time for me to move on."

Donovan knew Shaw's stomach must be turning. The Guild required that each crew have certain personnel employed. A mechanic was one of them. Why was it so hard to keep a mechanic?

"Well, it's obviously your decision to make, but I'm not gonna lie to you. This puts us in a bad spot with the Guild," Shaw said.

"I know. And I may have a solution. I know a man in Port Frisco. Great mechanic. If you hire him, you won't have to report to the Guild that you don't have one," Foster said.

"We still have to report your departure to them. We can't keep our license with the Guild if we don't have a mechanic onboard," Shaw said.

"Trust me, Captain. My guy is really good. You can just report to the Guild that you've replaced your mechanic."

Donovan knew Shaw didn't really have a choice. He couldn't make Foster stay. Last time Shaw had to replace someone, the Guild gave him two weeks to do it. During that time, the *Crash Wagon*'s license was suspended until a replacement was hired. If a replacement wasn't found within the two week period, Shaw would've lost his license with the Guild. They would've taken the RAID from the ship, and if he wanted back in, he would've had to reapply for the license.

"What's your guy's name?" Shaw asked.

"Daniel Vesh."

Shaw rubbed his temples with the tips of his fingers. "Can you get word to him? Let him know we're heading that way?"

"Yes, sir."

"Okay. Get us a time and place to meet him. We should be arriving in a couple days."

"I'll handle it, Captain," Foster said.

"Until then, I've given you some meds that will help with the swelling in your knee," Donovan said. "They will make you sleepy. You need to get some rest."

"Sure thing, Doc," Foster said.

Shaw left the infirmary, clearly with a lot on his mind. The only thing that was on Donovan's mind was a cup of coffee. Now. Where did he leave his coffee cup?

* * *

When Brett walked into the shuttle bay, Jordan was leaning against the shuttle, holding a digital tablet.

"I think we're getting a little low on hydraulic fluid," Brett said.

"Do you want me to do the inventory or not?" Jordan said.

"Okay. What's up with you?"

"What are you talking about? You told me to check the inventory. I'm checking the inventory."

"You know what I'm talking about."

"I'm just a little stressed, okay? I'm allowed to be a little stressed, right?"

"Yes, Jordan. You're allowed to be a little stressed. What you're not allowed to do is snap at the captain like you did."

"I didn't snap. I just got a little frustrated. Am I not allowed to do that either?"

Brett was now the one getting frustrated. "Okay. Fine. You got a little frustrated. Happens to all of us. The only difference being, the rest of us usually have something that causes the frustration. Is there something you're not telling me?"

Jordan looked down at the tablet. "Are you happy here?"

"What do you mean?"

"I mean I'm starting to feel burned out. Seven years, Brett. We've been on this ship for seven years. We've never been on a ship half that long before."

"The others weren't like this one."

"What makes this one so special?"

He had never had to verbalize what he liked about being part of the *Crash Wagon* crew before. He thought it all the time, but it felt a little strange to say it out loud. He shouldn't have to. Jordan should know already.

"This one is family."

"No. Our family is back at Laguerto."

"You saying you want to go back there? To that life?"

"Of course not. But, like it or not, that's our family. You can't just replace them with another group of people. This crew is great. The best we've ever worked with by a long shot. But if you're relying on them to be there for you when you really need them, don't. I'm not saying they would ever do anything to hurt us, but don't expect them to stick their neck out for us. Sometimes I think you trust them too much."

"Do you think that maybe you're acting a little paranoid?"

"Paranoid?"

"That's right. You seem to have forgotten that for seven years Shaw has made sure we were taken care of."

"But will he be there when things get bad?"

"He's never given me a reason to believe otherwise."

"I really like these people. I do. I'm just saying we have to be careful about trusting them too much. It's come back to bite us before. As much as you might like to think they are, they aren't family."

"What about Jaimie?"

"What about her?"

"She's doesn't have any blood relation to anyone on the ship."

"And?"

"How does Shaw treat her?" Brett saw the moment his sister realized he had just made a point she wouldn't be able to successfully argue. "Shaw treats that girl like she's his own daughter. He treats you the same. You may not see it, or want to see it, but he does."

Jordan turned her attention back to the tablet. Brett reached out and took it from her. She continued to stare down at her hands.

"I know it's hard. You and I, we've had a difficult life to say the least. But we have finally found something good, Jordan. You don't trust them because you're used to people not being trustworthy. You're feeling paranoid because you're used to bad things happening to you. But you trust me, right?"

She looked up at him. "You know I do."

"Then you need to trust me when I tell you that this is where we need to be. Right here. On this ship. With this crew. Okay?"

Jordan nodded. "Okay. I'll get it together. I'll be fine."

"Good. Just try to remember. We have it pretty good. Not all crews are like this."

Chapter 3

The landing gear of the small transport was damaged on take-off from Red Bay, Mars' largest city. Terry reluctantly told Captain Pella he could only re-wire part of it from the inside while in flight. The rest had to be done on the outside, and there was no way he was putting on a suit and going out there. No way. Not Terry Shannon. After explaining to the captain that, because of this, the landing struts on the port side would only descend half-way, she seemed disappointed. He knew he had better start looking for work when they reached their destination. Captain Pella had hinted to him before that she had no use for a mechanic that was scared to spacewalk. He figured that's why they were making the unexpected stop in Port Frisco. It almost rivaled Port of Orleans as far as finding crew went.

When *Pella's Bell* approached its designated dock, the two starboard side struts touched down gently, but the port ones only lowered halfway down, and the ship lurched hard to the left, giving everything and everyone a good jolt. Once the ship settled, Terry saw Captain Pella walking toward him. He had seen that look on her face before. She was upset.

He stood to face her, ran his hands through his blond hair, attempting to make it presentable, and gave her his patented smile. "Sorry, Captain. Now that we're landed, I'll go on out and take care of the outside wiring. I just need—"

"No," the captain interrupted. "You won't."

"It's probably not that bad. I'm sure the damage isn't major. I'll just take a look."

Pella shook her head. "You're fired, Terry. Get off my ship."

He knew it was coming, but he gave a show anyway. "What? I told you this would happen!"

"And, I told you, if you couldn't spacewalk, I had no need for you!"

"Is that what this is about?"

"I've tried to show you in the past. Several times, actually. Remember New London? I couldn't even get you to put on the suit!"

"Don't you know how dangerous that is? What if the

suit had a...leak?"

"We were on the ground, Terry!"

"Yeah...well...still."

"I gave you a chance. Get off my ship."

He saw that she was serious. No sense in wasting time. He gathered his things into a bag and left.

* * *

Terry had been in The Crewman Saloon many times before. One time, he'd gotten his nose broken there. The last time, his crew was celebrating the delivery of a shipment of pure ice from Mars. They managed to lose only seventeen percent of it to melting. It was a huge delivery and a huge payday. This time, he simply sat and drank. He was a little tipsy. 'Drunk' would be the word.

He took another drink of his beer. "And then," he said to the bartender, "she said...'Get off of the ship that is mine...and...not yours, you non-spacewalking, yet somewhat attractive, moron!' Wait. I think that's what she said," Terry put his head face-down on the bar. "I'll have to ask her next time I see her. I can't remember real good right now."

"You do realize that's the third time you've told that story tonight?" the bartender asked. "You got anything else to talk about? Or, maybe you'd just like to drink... quietly?"

"This bar smells funny," Terry said. "Hey, Sal! How

do you get funny-smelling wood? I've always wondered."

"I'm sure there are many things in this bar's history that would explain why it smells, sweetie," a woman's voice said.

Terry lifted his head and saw a young woman standing next to him. She was very beautiful. She had her black hair pulled back in a ponytail and smelled like strawberries.

"What'll it be, Miss?" the bartender asked.

"I'll have what he's having."

"I'll have what I'm having too," Terry said. He turned back to the woman. "I'm Terry."

"Hello, Terry. I'm Jaimie."

"I know who you are."

"You do? How?"

"You just told me."

Jaimie laughed at his attempt to make a joke. "Funny guy."

The bartender brought Terry and Jaimie their beer. He handed Jaimie's to her with a smile. When he turned to Terry the smile faded. Terry reached for the beer, but the bartender set it on the bar, just out of reach.

"Sal's a funny guy," Terry said, leaning over to get it. "So, would you care to drink with me?"

"Sorry," Jaimie said. "I'm actually working. It was nice meeting you." She started to walk away.

"So, you're a prostitute?" he asked.

She stopped dead in her tracks, turned and walked

back to him. "You think I'm a prostitute? Do I look like a prostitute?"

He realized from the look on her face that he may have jumped to his conclusion a little too quickly. "No! I just...Well, you're in a bar...and you said you were working...so..." He turned away from her and took a drink from his beer. "Prostitute," he said under his breath, looking at her out of the corner of his eye.

"I'm a pilot," Jaimie said.

"Yeah! No! That's what I meant! Pilot," Terry said. The last thing he wanted to do was offend this girl.

"Uh huh," Jaimie said. She gave him a sideways look.

"Sorry. I didn't mean anything by it."

She smiled. "It's okay. You're drunk. If you weren't, I'd sock you."

"You'd 'sock' me? Is that a prostitute term?"

"Hey!"

"I'm joking! It was a joke!"

"Well, stop. I don't like that."

"I'm sorry. Really. So, how are you working here tonight?"

"See those two over there?" She pointed at a man and woman sitting at a table across the room.

"Yeah."

"That's Brett and his sister, Jordan. We're meeting someone about joining our crew."

Terry perked up a little more. He needed a job. He tried to focus. "Your crew? You mean like a ship crew?"

"Yeah. I'm the pilot on a rescue ship." She took a drink of her beer.

"What's it like working on a rescue ship?"

"I love it. Some days are a little more exciting than others. But, we're helping people. It's a good gig."

"So. My taxes pay your wages, right?"

"That's right."

"Well, it's probably only right for you to show your appreciation by buying me a beer, right?"

"Really? Cause, you have like seven in front of you."

"But, I want eight."

"No, sweetie. You don't need eight."

"Fine. But, let me ask you this. Just out of curiosity, what does the job entail?"

"Well. It's pretty simple actually. People send out a distress signal. If we pick it up, we go try to help them."

"Do you haul cargo?"

"Nope."

"Really? So, you all just get a salary?"

"Not exactly. We get paid based on what each job entailed. For example, we get paid more for saving people than repairing a ship. If we can save lives, and get their ship up and running, that's a good payday. Plus, there's bonuses. There's a bonus for being the first on the scene, as well as being the only ship on the scene. Sometimes, a rescue ship is asked to escort another ship just in case problems occur. The ship being escorted might be carrying precious cargo, like pure ice, or some political figure."

"Interesting. So, who are you and your friends meeting with?" Terry took a drink of his beer.

"We're looking to replace our mechanic."

He spit his beer out on the bartender's shirt. Sal looked like he was going to beat him to death with a whiskey bottle. Terry quickly wiped his mouth with the back of his sleeve. "I'm a mechanic!"

"I thought you were a drunk," Jaimie said.

"I'm a drunk mechanic. But I'll just be a mechanic tomorrow. I could really use a job."

"Well. I hear prostitutes do pretty good around here."

"Come on!"

"Sorry, sweetie. Like I said, we're already meeting with someone."

"I'm better than whoever you're looking to hire."

"You think so?"

"How many people do you know that can rewire a ground lock?"

"None."

"I can."

"Aw, sweetie," Jaimie said, as she pinched Terry's cheek. "No, you can't."

"I can!"

Jaimie saw Brett signaling her. The man they were meeting with had just arrived. "I have to go. We're escorting him back to the ship to meet the captain."

Terry saw the mechanic who was with them. "That's

the guy you're thinking about hiring?" he asked in a loud voice that carried across the bar. "I doubt he'd know his way around a bottle opener, much less an accelerator core."

Brett and Jordan turned around and glared at him.

"Really?" Brett asked.

"We can hear you," Jordan said.

Jaimie closed her eyes, her expression pained. When she opened them, she smiled at Terry.

"It was nice meeting you. Good luck finding a job. Also, good luck dealing with what I can only imagine will be the mother of all hangovers in the morning."

Terry was disappointed. "Yeah. It was nice meeting you, too." He turned back to his beer.

A moment later, he heard the sound of chair legs as they slid across the floor. When he looked over, he saw Jaimie and her companions moving towards the front door. Jaimie smiled and waved at him on her way out. He waved back, then finished his beer.

"I'm out, Sal," Terry said. "I need another one."

"Listen, pal. I think you've had enough."

Terry shot him a look. "Oh come on, Sal! I can drink more and more!"

"Would you stop calling me 'Sal'! That's not my name!"

"I know. It just sounds like a great bartender name. I once saw a play that had a bartender named Mortimer. It's like 'Sal', but it was 'Mortimer'. I think it's spelled different. He was a funny bartender, and he—"

The bartender took Terry by the arm. "You need a place to stay tonight?"

"That's an affirmatory, Sparky."

The bartender sighed. "Fine. We have a few rooms open upstairs. I won't even charge you for the night if you just go to bed. Now."

"Aw, Sal. After all we've been through, you're still there to lend a helping hand. There is just one more thing I need to ask for you to do for me from you."

"What?"

"I may need you to carry me. It's strange, but I don't think I can feel my legs. Or ears."

He passed out.

Chapter 4

Donovan examined the readouts on his digital physician's chart. Daniel Vesh appeared to be in good health. His blood pressure was a little higher than normal, but Donovan attributed that to being in a new place and having a new job. There was nothing to indicate he would not be fit to perform his duties. At least from a medical standpoint.

"Is all of this really necessary, Doc?" Vesh asked.

"Absolutely not," Donovan said. "In fact, the entire medical profession is a complete and total waste of time. Also, there are little green men that live beneath the surface of Mars, and unicorns are real."

"I feel fine, Doc."

Those were four words that Donovan had heard his entire practice. Whether employed with a hospital or as part of a crew on a ship, one thing remained the same. No one ever felt they needed a medical examination unless they were obviously sick or injured. On many occasions, the patient was very surprised at what Donovan found during the exam. Whether it was a tumor in its beginning stages of growth, or one of the new diseases that originated on Mars, the patient always started out feeling fine.

"I'm sure you do. Now, please remove your shirt."

"My shirt? What for?"

"Mr. Vesh. I am this vessel's physician. I am paid well to do my job. Please do not prevent me from performing my duties."

"Well, I am this vessel's patient and I have a right to know what this vessel's physician is doing."

"Very well. I need you to remove your shirt so that I may take a bio scan. The scan will record data such as blood pressure, blood type, body fat percentage, muscle mass, bone density, etc. This is information that the Guild requires of new employees."

"Fantastic. Can I ask a favor?"

"I can't currently think of a reason why you can't."

"I've got a tattoo between my shoulder blades. I'd kind of like it to stay between us. You know. Doctor-patient confidentiality?"

"It's not a unicorn, is it? Because my comment earlier

was a joke."

"Doc, I'm serious. A few years back, I was in a relationship with this girl. I was crazy about her. She was really into ancient markings and symbols. It was kind of her thing. She talked me into getting a tattoo of one of her favorite symbols. Couple days later, she dumped me. Turns out, it was all over a bet she had with her friends as to whether or not she could get a guy to get a tattoo. It's a little humiliating. So please, not a word."

"Not a problem. Your secret is safe with me. Now please, remove your shirt."

Vesh took his shirt off. The tattoo was an ancient Chinese symbol. It wasn't the first tattoo of that kind Donovan had seen on a patient. Many people seem to like words and symbols from ancient cultures tattooed on their bodies. He never understood why someone would want to brand themselves in such a way. Then again, love can be a powerful motivator. Even if it does turn out to be a simple case of infatuation.

Donovan used the bio scanner to scan Vesh's vitals and other information into a file format that could be transmitted to the Guild. They were very thorough when it came to keeping accurate employee records. Donovan assumed it had something to do with the possibility of an audit from the Central Government. The Guild had a very good thing going. They wouldn't want to do anything that would jeopardize it.

"Now then. That was painless, wasn't it? I'll make

sure this data gets to Ms. Ellis on the bridge so she can send it to the Guild."

"I'm going there now. Want me to take it to her?"

"If you wouldn't mind," Donovan handed Vesh the digital chart. "I'm exhausted, and it's late. If she's already retired for the evening, just bring it back to the infirmary and lay it on my desk, please."

"No problem, Doc," Vesh slid off the exam table and onto his feet. "Remember. The tattoo is our secret."

"My lips are sealed, Mr. Vesh."

* * *

Jaimie sat at the console on the bridge, covered in a blanket. She had begun to doze and thought maybe she should make her way to her bunk and get some sleep. There was no reason for her to be at the helm. The *Crash Wagon* was safely docked at Port Frisco. But there was something comforting about being in her pilot's chair. She glanced over all the different switches and dials on the main console and thought about how many times she'd used them to save someone's life.

Her mind drifted to the man she met at the bar earlier that night. Terry. She thought about the horrible hangover he was going to have in the morning. A small grin tugged the corner of her mouth.

"Jaimie?"

Startled, she turned to see that Vesh had entered the

bridge. Over the years, she had developed an ability to know when someone was coming up behind her, but she hadn't heard him approach. Maybe she was more tired than she thought.

She pulled a stray lock of hair out of her face. "Daniel? What can I do for you?"

"I'm sorry. I didn't mean to scare you. The doc just finished looking me over."

"Did he do the bio scan?"

"Right here." Vesh held up the digital chart, then handed it to her.

She took it from him. She had an interest in medical work. She liked visiting with Donovan when he wasn't too busy. He let her help him in the past with minor procedures such as cleaning and wrapping small wounds. "Isn't the bio scan cool?"

"Yeah. It was super fun."

Jaimie picked up on the sarcasm. "I'm serious. Dr. Barrett is teaching me how to do it." She turned and plugged the chart into the main console. After flipping a few switches, the word 'Sending' flashed on the screen.

"You want to be a doctor?" Vesh asked.

"No. Not really. But I want to learn some of the basic things he does. He's teaching me a little here and there so I can help him out if needed."

She watched the screen until she received confirmation that the Guild mainframe had recorded Vesh's medical record. 'Transmission Complete' flashed on the screen. Jaimie disconnected the chart and handed it back to Vesh. "All done."

"Good. Guess I'll drop this off at the infirmary a little later. In the meantime, I'd like to get a look under the helm. I want to start familiarizing myself with the ship's systems."

"Now? It's awfully late."

"I'm kind of a night owl. I like working when there's no distractions."

Jaimie got up and wrapped the blanket around her. "Knock yourself out. I think everyone else has gone to bed, or is on their way. I know I am. Guess I'll see you in the morning."

"Goodnight," Vesh said.

"Goodnight."

Jaimie made her way to her bunk. Its walls were decorated with postcards she collected from the different cities and stations she had been to while on the *Crash Wagon*. Beside her bed was a night stand with a lamp and a framed photo of her parents and little brother. On her bed lay an empty box that once contained strawberries. She tossed the box on the floor, too tired to take it to the galley disposal bin. She turned her lamp off and fell into bed. A small smile formed as she drifted off to sleep, thinking of that drunk blond-headed mechanic she met earlier and the hangover that was coming to him in the morning.

* * *

Jordan sat in her bunk. She had several handguns spread out on a wooden desk. Most were disassembled. She very carefully cleaned the components. She was good at taking care of her belongings, especially her firearms. She learned to take apart and reassemble guns at a very early age. While most little girls were playing with dolls and having pretend tea parties, she was cleaning guns and shooting targets at the firing range. Those skills had kept her and Brett employed much better than serving make believe tea would have.

There was a knock on her door.

"Yes?"

"It's Shaw."

What did he want at this time of night? He hadn't said anything about her outburst in the galley a few days ago. Maybe the captain had finally decided to bring it up.

"Come in."

The door opened and he stepped into Jordan's bunk.

"Is everything okay?" Jordan asked. "I thought everyone was asleep."

"They are. I just saw your light on, so I figured I'd check with you on our inventory. Were you able to get us restocked?"

"Yeah. For the most part. I couldn't find any of the strawberries that Jaimie likes."

"Well. Looks like you might have a feisty, strawberry-deprived brunette on your hands."

Jordan smiled at the mental image. "Probably. But I can handle it."

"Okay. Well, goodnight." He turned to walk out of Jordan's bunk.

"Sir?"

He stopped and turned back around. "Yes?"

Jordan paused. She had rarely ever felt guilt for things she had done. She did, however, feel a responsibility to the crew and its captain.

"About the other day, when I argued your decision to come here." She paused again and glanced at Shaw, expecting him to say something.

"Yes?"

"Oh. I kind of thought you were going to interrupt me and say something like, 'Don't worry about it.' or 'It's no big deal.' You know. Something like that."

"I wasn't going to do that."

"You know what? It's not important. Never mind."

"Well, hang on now. You opened this can. Let's get everything out."

Jordan exhaled. She regretted bringing the subject up. "I thought we were making a mistake in bypassing King's Bay for Port Frisco. I made you aware of my thoughts on the matter. I should've let it go after that, but I didn't. I've just been a little on edge the last few days. Stress, I guess. Maybe we were in deep space too long without a break. I'm sorry if I was being difficult."

"You mean more difficult than usual?"

"Yes, sir," Jordan said, slightly amused. "More than usual."

"How old are you, Jordan?"

"You know how old I am."

"Yeah, but I'm asking you anyway. How old?"

Jordan wondered where he was going with this. "Twenty-eight."

"Now, I'd be willing to bet a bottle of my best whiskey that, despite your age, you're better at this job than others that have more experience than you. That being said, you're still young. What you need to understand is that even though you may see me as an old-timer, I'm still very good at this captain thing. My priority is the well-being of my crew, my ship, and the people we manage to rescue. Being part of my crew puts you at the top of the list. Getting those people here to Port Frisco didn't hurt us, and it was a big help to them. So, even though I do encourage the crew to speak their mind, I also need them to trust that I'm going to do what's best."

She recalled the conversation she had with Brett in the shuttle bay a couple days ago. He, too, had asked her to try to trust the captain a little more. She figured she should probably make the effort. "I understand. I'm sorry I was being difficult."

"Well, I wouldn't worry too much about it, Jordan. In all honesty, I'd be worried if you started agreeing with me too much. That's when we'll know there's a problem."

"I suppose you're right, sir."

"Don't stay up all night cleaning them guns now. Get some sleep." Shaw turned and left.

"Goodnight, sir."

She picked up one of the handguns and began cleaning again. She stopped and put it back down. She was tired. The guns could wait. She organized the parts according to which gun they belonged to and turned her desk lamp off. She walked to her dresser, opened it, and grabbed a tank top and a pair of cotton shorts. Before she could change, however, she heard the comm box in her bunk buzz. She walked over to it and pressed the 'talk' button.

"Yes?"

"Hawkins. This is Vesh. I was wondering if you could go to the shuttle bay and give me a hand," came the reply.

"What are you doing working so late? Everyone else is asleep. Is there a problem with the shuttle?"

"I just wanted to check the shuttle's RAID control receivers before I went to bed. I'll send a RAID signal from the bridge. All I need you to do is make sure the shuttle receives it. Easy."

"This can't wait until morning?"

"We're taking off in the morning. I would hate for something to happen where we need to transfer control to the shuttle, and we can't. Wouldn't look very good on me, being my first day. It'll only take a second."

"Fine. I'm on my way to the shuttle bay. I'll let you

know when I'm in position."

"Thanks. I'll owe you one."

She slipped into her boots, grabbed a mobile comm box, and left her bunk.

* * *

Jordan stepped into the shuttle bay and threw the light switch. The lights sprung to life with a distinct hum. The shuttle bay always smelled like grease and oil. She made her way over to the *Crash Wagon*'s shuttle and keyed in a code on its doors that would allow her access. The key panel made a beep, which indicated the code she used was accepted. The doors opened.

Jordan was surprised to see Vesh on the other side. Before she could ask why he wasn't on the bridge, he drove his left foot into her gut, knocking her backwards. Her mobile comm fell from her grasp.

She managed to catch her breath around the same time she felt adrenaline rush through her body, anticipating the fight. The trick was controlling the adrenaline. Not letting it overtake you.

Vesh stepped out of the shuttle and walked toward her. He had a stunner in his right hand. She'd need to try to avoid that.

"What are you doing!"

"My job."

He lunged at her with the stunner. She dropped to

her back and kicked both feet into his stomach, forcing him backwards. This gave her the time she needed to get to her feet and into a defensive stance.

He was faster than she thought, though. He recovered and thrust the stunner at her again. Jordan deflected his right arm and landed a blow to his nose with her right fist. She knew from the sound that she had broken it. Vesh dropped the stunner and clapped his hands to his face.

Jordan bent down to pick it up, but he grabbed a handful of her hair, drove his left knee into her gut, forcing the wind from her lungs. He yanked her backwards by her hair and threw her down, slamming her head against the steel deck.

Her head rang and tunnel vision was setting in. Vesh was probably going for the stunner. There wasn't a lot of time. She had to get up. As she did, his hand closed around her throat. He drove her head back down hard against the deck.

She felt the cold metal tip of the stunner press against her chest. In the instant before it was activated, all Jordan could think of was how Brett had apparently never got around to explaining his 'crew is family' concept to Vesh.

Then...blackness.

Chapter 5

Terry was sleeping in one of the rooms above The Crewman Saloon, when a splash of cold water brought him upright, coughing and sputtering. His head pounded like someone had taken a hammer to it.

"Wake up."

He opened his eyes and let the unforgiving light in. He saw two people standing at the foot of his bed. He recognized them from the night before. Not the new mechanic and the sister - the other two. Jaimie. And what was the man's name? Brian? Brandon? Brisco?

"I don't remember ordering room service," he said.

"This isn't room service," the man said. "It's a wake up call. Get dressed and come downstairs." He threw

Terry's shirt at him, hitting him in the face.

"Stop throwing things at me!" Terry said. He rubbed his head. "Oh, that was too loud."

* * *

When he came downstairs, the wooden treads creaked under each step, the sound attacking his headache with sonic precision. He saw Jaimie at the bar with her companion standing close by. Behind the bar was the bartender from the night before, pouring a cup of coffee. Other than that, the place was empty. It was far too early for patrons to be filling the chairs. Jaimie motioned for him to come over. He wasn't sure what was going on. He also wasn't sure he cared to find out. The only thing he knew he wanted was to find some relief for his hangover. He made his way to where they sat.

"Morning, sunshine," Jaimie said. "Have a seat. I've ordered a coffee for you."

He took a seat. "Thanks." He rubbed his eyes, as if that would somehow massage his headache away.

The bartender brought the cup of coffee. He set it down in front of him and leaned in close to Terry's ear. "Enjoy!"

Terry grimaced in pain. "Really? Was that necessary?"

"Oh, absolutely," the bartender said. He walked to the back of the bar and began cleaning glasses.

The stranger leaned against the bar and looked from Terry to Jaimie. "Can we move things along here?"

"I've got this," Jaimie said.

Terry's face was in his hands. "Can someone tell me what is going on?"

Jaimie moved his hands. "Do you remember me from last night?"

"Did something happen between us? Cause if so, the smiley face tattoo on my right hip is from a bet I lost. Just so you know."

"Good to know. But nothing like that happened."

"Are you sure? Cause you were pretty wasted last night," Terry said.

"I think you're confusing me with you," she said.

The man got in Terry's face. "Listen. I hate to break up your little fantasy here, and I'm truly sorry about your tattoo, but we are in a real big hurry."

Terry wasn't in a good mood and this guy wasn't making it any better. "Could you get out of my face? I don't even know your name."

"I'm Brett Hawkins."

"Terry Shannon."

"Well then. I'm glad we cleared that up," Brett said.

"Terry. Look at me," Jaimie said. "Last night, you told me that you can rewire a ground lock."

"I'm sure I said a lot of things last night."

"I'm sure you say a lot of things a lot of times," Brett added, under his breath.

"I heard that," Terry said.

"Terry. We need you to focus, okay?" Jaimie said. "Here's the bottom line. The woman that was here with us last night - that was Jordan Hawkins. Do you remember me pointing her out? She's Brett's sister. The mechanic we hired has taken her."

That woke him up. "How do you know she didn't just leave?" Terry straightened and pointed at Brett. "If he was my brother, I would just leave."

"They were both gone this morning, and so is our shuttle. We found blood on the bay deck. All of Jordan's handguns are in her room. She wouldn't have left without taking at least one of them," Jaimie said.

"She wouldn't have left without telling me either," Brett said.

Terry's mechanic instincts began to settle in. "Can't you track the shuttle?"

"Yes. But he put a ground lock on our ship. We contacted the port authority and they said there's nothing they can do; the ground lock was initiated from inside our ship."

"So you want me to try to break the lock?"

"Here's the deal. You break the ground lock, and the mechanic job is yours," Brett said.

This was exactly the opportunity Terry needed. Could he lift the ground lock? Who knew? But he decided he was going to try. He needed the job.

He stood up, took a drink from his cup of coffee, and

slammed the mug down on the bar, accidentally shattering it into a million ceramic pieces.

"Get out!" the bartender yelled.

Terry grabbed his head. "Too loud."

* * *

Brett, Jaimie, and Terry were on the bridge. Terry and Jaimie were under the main console, trying to rewire the ground lock. Brett was leaning against a computer bank, when he wasn't pacing.

Terry had a small data pad linked into the ship's console. He studied the data as it scrolled across the small screen. Jaimie lay on the deck beside him and held a flashlight. She was an interesting one. He could tell she loved her job. Being a pilot required a very complex skill set, so obviously she was very intelligent. But, what stood out about her the most was her ability to find interest and joy in anything. She seemed just as content to be lying on the deck, holding a flashlight as he imagined she was at the helm of the ship.

"You understand all that stuff on the screen?" she asked.

"It's not so much about understanding it as it is recognizing a pattern," Terry said.

"What kind of pattern?"

"It's hard to explain. The landing dock is tied in to the port authority. It's communicating back and forth with the ship. The ship sends information such as the ship's weight, as well as make and class."

"All of this I know."

"But, smarty pants, the ground lock is telling the ship it can't leave. Most of the time, the port authority tells a ship it can't leave when they have a reason to hold it. But, in this case, the ship is telling the landing platform that it can't leave. It's backwards. The ground lock was initiated from the ship. I'm looking for the pattern in the communication that tells the ship it has to stay put."

"Then what?"

"Then, we interrupt that pattern and break the sequence that's keeping the ship locked to the landing platform."

Terry heard someone else walk onto the bridge.

"That's all well and good, son. But, are you sure you'll be able to do all that? There's not many people who have."

Terry slid out from under the console. He was getting a little annoyed at all the pessimism. He had been woken up with a splash of cold water to the face. He was currently suffering from what should be medically classified as a mega hangover. In addition to all of that, he wasn't getting any support from the people he was trying to help.

Well. He couldn't say he wasn't getting any support. Jaimie was great.

The comment came from an older man with a mostly

bald head. He still had some silver hair above each ear, but not much.

"Listen, Gramps. I've come here to help you all out," Terry said.

"Um…" Jaimie quickly slid out from under the console and sat up. "Terry."

"I know you're in a hurry. But I need to be able to do this without being questioned the whole time!" Terry continued.

Jaimie tried to cut him off. "Terry, this is—"

"The last thing I need is some aging—"

"Terry!" Jaimie yelled, finally getting his attention. "This is Captain Joseph Shaw."

Terry's eyes widened. "Captain?"

"Yeah. I like 'Captain' better than 'Gramps'," Shaw said.

Good work, Shannon. Nothing helped to nail down a job better than calling your prospective employer insulting names. Terry felt awkward. He needed to try to divert the attention off of himself.

He pointed at Brett. "He threw water on me."

From the look the captain leveled at him, he thought he may have just made his situation worse.

"Did he now?" Shaw said. "Well, I'll tell you what. If you help us get out of this ground lock problem, maybe I can help. I'm not promising anything, but I'm thinking I can get you a towel, or maybe even another shirt."

Yeah. He'd made his situation worse.

"Yes, sir," he said quietly. He slid back under the console.

"Don't worry, Captain. Terry can do this, I'm sure of it," Jaimie said. She rejoined him with an amused look.

"He threw water on me? Smooth."

"I panicked."

"Whatever. You found the pattern yet?"

"Not yet. I'm getting there. I just need a little quiet now, please."

"Okay. No problem."

A few moments passed without a sound. Then she said, "So. A smiley face tattoo on your hip, huh?"

"I lost a bet."

"So you've said. What was the bet?"

"What?"

"The bet you lost. What was the bet?"

"I bet someone I could do something. Turns out, I couldn't."

"Well? Come on. What was it you couldn't do?"

Terry had really been hoping this wasn't going to come up. Not now.

"This," he said.

"This what?"

Terry let out a sigh. "I bet someone I could lift a ground lock."

"Are you kidding me?"

"Keep your voice down."

"Terry. I vouched for you. I told them you could do

this. I bent over backwards to convince them to hire you," she said, in an angry whisper. "We took the time to come back to that bar to find you. I even begged them to offer you the mechanic job! And now you're telling me that you can't—"

"Could you hold that thought?" he interrupted. "I seem to have accessed the ground lock signal."

The small screen on his data pad indicated that the ground lock signal had been isolated.

"I knew you could do it!" she said. "Not only are you cute, you're a genius!"

"I told you I was better than that other mechanic," Terry said. "If you would've hired me in the first place, none of this—"

His data pad made a beeping sound. He looked at the screen and saw that a password was required to lift the ground lock.

"Oh."

"What?"

"It's asking for a password."

"Do you know the password?"

"I do not."

"Idiot!" Jaimie said as she slid out from under the console.

"What happened to cute genius?" he called after her.

"Just transfer your data pad screen to the main console."

He transferred the data, disconnected his data pad,

and slid out from under the console.

Shaw, Brett, Terry, and Jaimie all stared at the screen. A single password stood between the ground lock and freedom.

Even though they weren't in the clear yet, Terry was a little proud of what he had done. There weren't many people that could isolate a ground lock signal, and he knew it. Still, he was in a room with three very disappointed people. This wasn't a game to see if he could isolate a signal. This was a practical application. Brett's sister was in trouble.

"Sorry, Captain."

"Nothing to be sorry about, son," Shaw said. "You got us this far, which is something most people wouldn't have been able to do. If you want the mechanic job, it's yours."

Now he felt even worse about insulting Shaw. The captain was a fair man. He was going to make sure he never made Shaw regret his decision to hire him.

"Thank you, sir. I appreciate it."

"Does anyone have any idea what this password could be?" Shaw asked.

"Vesh set the password when he set up the ground lock, right? What would he have been thinking about?" Brett asked.

Jaimie entered the name 'Daniel Vesh' into the console. It didn't work.

"Guess that would've been too easy," she said.

Shaw walked over to the comm box. He pressed a button on it. "Doctor?"

"Yes, Captain?" Donovan's voice was heard through the comm speaker on the bridge.

"Come to the bridge, please."

"On my way."

Shaw made his way back. "I figure since the Doc examined him, maybe he knows a little more about him than we do."

Terry realized he was about to meet another member of the crew. Of his crew. He wondered what the doctor might be like. So far he was pleased with his new workmates, for the most part. Shaw seemed like he would be a fine captain to work for.

He still wasn't sure about Brett, the first mate, but he decided to give him the benefit of the doubt, seeing that his sister had been kidnapped. He had only seen her across the bar. Jaimie told him her name was Jordan, and she was Brett's younger sister. Kind of a tough girl. Given the circumstances, Terry hoped he would get a chance to meet her.

Then, there was Jaimie. Terry really liked her. She had a very cheerful and bubbly personality. She seemed to be very enthusiastic in everything she did. He'd get along with her just fine.

Jaimie pulled up Vesh's records. She entered his birthday as the password. Again, it failed.

"Try it backwards," Terry said.

Jaimie inputted Vesh's name backwards. Nothing. She tried his birthday. Again, the attempt failed.

Donovan entered the bridge. "Did our new grease monkey lift the ground lock?"

"He got us a good chunk of the way there," Shaw said. "Apparently, the signal is password protected. I figured maybe you could help us guess the password since you talked to him a while in your examination."

"Well, I shall certainly try, Captain," Donovan said.

"I think if I would've gotten this far, back when I made the bet, it would've been enough to not have to get my smiley face tattoo," Terry said.

"I'm sure it's adorable," Jaimie said.

"Ms. Ellis," Donovan said. "Try different variations of the word 'king' or 'royalty', please."

Brett looked at Donovan. "What makes you guess that, Doctor?"

"The mention of—" Donovan paused. "I apologize, but I haven't been properly introduced to our newest mechanic."

"Terry Shannon," Terry said.

"The mention of Mr. Shannon's adorable tattoo recalls to mind a tattoo that our previous mechanic has between his shoulder blades. He asked me to keep it secret, but given our current circumstances—"

Brett stepped in closer to Donovan. "What was the tattoo?"

Terry felt the tension rising in the room and

wondered what that was about.

"It was a Chinese symbol. I'm not an expert, but I believe it is a symbol that means 'king' or 'royalty'," Donovan said.

"Jaimie," Brett said, still staring at Donovan. "Try 'Monarchy'."

Jaimie entered the word into the password field. The words 'Ground Lock Lifted' appeared on the screen.

"That's it! It's lifted!" Jaimie crowed. She threw her arms in the air and turned to face her crew mates. "I knew Terry would do it! I knew he could—"

Brett grabbed Donovan by the collar and slammed him against the wall. "Why didn't you mention the tattoo in your report?"

"Unhand me, Hawkins!" Donovan demanded.

Shaw pulled Brett off of him. "Let him go!"

Brett held his hands up to show his assault was done and took a deep breath. "Why did you leave the tattoo out of your physical evaluation report, Doctor?"

Donovan straightened his collar. "Mr. Vesh asked me to keep it between us. He evoked his doctor-patient confidentiality right."

"Well, if I had known about the tattoo, none of this would've happened. That tattoo is the mark of The Monarchy. They're a mob family."

"What does the mob want with Jordan?" Shaw asked.

"We need to go, now," Brett said. "I'll explain everything on the way. But we need to get moving."

Shaw looked at Brett for a moment. "Jaimie. Where have you tracked our shuttle to?"

"Port of Orleans, sir," Jaimie said.

"Set a course," Shaw said. "Then, everyone meet in the galley. Brett has a story to tell."

* * *

The crew was gathered around the large wooden table in the galley. All attention was on Brett Hawkins. It made him a little uncomfortable. It shouldn't, of course. He'd known everyone there for years. Well, except Terry. But, there was nothing intimidating about that goofy blond-headed mechanic. Still, he had to give him a little credit. Terry Shannon had done something that not many people could in breaking that ground lock. Plus, it got them one step closer to finding Jordan. It was time to come clean.

"Seven years ago, Jordan and I met with Captain Shaw," Brett said. "We've been on his crew ever since. It's a good crew. Good job. Before that, things weren't so good for me and Jordan. We sort of hopped from ship to ship for a couple years, not really fitting in. Truth be told, I never had a problem fitting in. But Jordan, well, it was a struggle for her. Still is sometimes, as I'm sure some of you know."

Brett took a drink from his beer bottle, then paused before continuing. "You see, before all the ship hopping, we worked for our father. He was not a good man. He had a small crime ring that he controlled out of Laguerto. That's where Jordan and I are from. It's where we grew up."

"Your dad was a mob boss?" Shaw asked.

Brett nodded. "Still is, as far as I know." He took another drink. "New Year's Eve, some men from The Monarchy mob family were in our territory, looking to make a name for themselves. Jordan and I warned them. Told them to leave. One of them drew on me. I hesitated. Wasn't ready. Fortunately, Jordan drew faster. Some of our guys showed up and the shooting started. Most of the Monarchy boys ran. We found out later that the guy Jordan had killed was the son of the Monarchy family head. I knew we weren't safe after that. Jordan and I wanted out of that life anyway. We wanted to get away from our father. So, we ran. This is where we ended up."

"So, you traded family loyalty for crew loyalty?" Donovan asked.

"Jordan and I had no intention of being criminals, and we surely had no intention on bringing any of this down on the crew," Brett said. "We hoped it would all just stay covered up in our past."

"Well then. I feel I must apologize for the role I played in all of this," Donovan said. "Mr. Hawkins, I can assure you that there will no longer be information withheld from either you or the Captain with regards to medical records."

"You saying you'll put the crew over your doctor-patient confidentiality?" Brett asked.

"Don't question my loyalty, Mr. Hawkins, and I won't question yours."

"Fair enough," Brett said.

Shaw stood up from the table. "Jaimie. Go to the bridge and make sure we're still tracking that shuttle. I want to know if it moves."

"Yes, sir," Jaimie said. She headed to the bridge.

"Terry," Shaw said. "Get to the engine room and see if we can't spare a little more power to the engines. Maybe we can make better time."

"I'm on it," Terry said. He, too, got up and left the galley.

"Any chance your old man might be willing to lend a hand?" Shaw asked Brett.

"Honestly? I'm surprised he hasn't come after me and Jordan himself. He wasn't very pleased when we left," Brett said. "What about the Guild?"

"Wouldn't do us any good. They'd just pull our license for not having a security officer. There's the Port of Orleans police."

"No good. The Monarchy probably owns half of it."

"I spoke to Jordan," Shaw said. "Last night, before going to bed. I explained to her that she was part of my crew and at the top of my priority list. I asked her to trust me. Now this happens."

"Wasn't your fault. And, for what it's worth, she does

trust you."

"Brett," Shaw said.

"Sir?"

"We're gonna get Jordan back."

Chapter 6

The *Crash Wagon* flew over Port of Orleans - not the largest port city on Earth, but arguably the busiest. It was also a hot spot for criminal activity. Sitting right on the southeastern coast of the continent, it was within a day's travel to Laguerto and Portozuela, two of the largest trafficking cities on Earth. There were places in Port of Orleans that were full of art, music, food, and culture. Because of this, tourism was a major part of its economy. Unfortunately, the crew would not be going to those parts of the city. The tracker on the shuttle showed that it was set down on the outskirts.

Jaimie landed the *Crash Wagon* at the docking station closest to the shuttle's tracking signal. The rest of the crew was gathered behind her on the bridge.

"Okay. We're gonna have to find some local transport to get us to the shuttle," Jaimie said.

Brett and Shaw were loading the clips into their handguns. Brett thought that given the part of town they were in, no one would notice them carrying any weapon they wanted. But they were trying to not draw attention. They just wanted to get in, get Jordan, and get out.

"Figured as much," Brett said. "That's why we're only carrying concealable weapons."

"Okay people. Listen up," Shaw said. "Brett, Terry, Jaimie, and I will make our way to the shuttle. Once we reach it, Terry and Jaimie are going to board and have it ready if we need to get out of there in a hurry. Brett and I will check the surrounding area."

"What do I do?" Donovan asked.

"You stay here on the *Wagon* and make sure the infirmary is ready in case we have injured," Shaw said. "Okay. Let's move."

* * *

Jordan was tied to a chair in the middle of a small room. It had windows, but the blinds were drawn shut. She could tell that wherever she was, it wasn't a ship. She heard footsteps coming toward the room. Daniel Vesh opened the door and walked in. He was carrying a bottle of water. His nose was bandaged from Jordan's punch in the shuttle bay.

He took a drink from the water bottle. "It's so hot here. I mean, it's hot out West too, but this is different, you know? It's dry out West. But here, it's the humidity that kills you, right?"

"You better hope the humidity is what kills you," Jordan said.

Vesh gave her a quick slap. "Hey! What have I been telling you about that mouth of yours?"

She stared back at him, unfazed by the slap and the metallic taste of blood from the corner of her mouth.

"Aw. What? You mad at me?" he asked. "Trust me. I'm treating you great compared to what the people coming to pick you up are known for."

"Yeah. Are you gonna tell me who's coming to get me, or is it safe for me to just continue to assume your cheese has finally slid off your cracker?"

"You haven't figured it out yet?"

"I really don't want to play guessing games with you."

"Here's a hint. The people coming to get you are taking you to Portozuela."

Jordan felt a cold sweat rush over her. "The Monarchy?"

"What's the matter? You don't look so tough now, girly. You look like you've seen a ghost. If you weren't unconscious when I brought you in here, you would've seen the markings on the outside of the building." He took another drink from the water bottle. "This is like, I don't know, one of their storage houses or something."

"Why didn't you just take me there?"

"All the way to Portozuela? Are you crazy? Not for what they're paying me. No, these Monarchy guys are really micromanaging this job. I was supposed to stay in Port Frisco until I was contacted. I was told I would be hired as a mechanic on your ship. Once there, I just ground lock the ship, load you onto the shuttle, and get you here, ready for retrieval."

"That plan seems a little far-fetched if you ask me."

Another man walked into the room. "Does it?"

Jordan couldn't believe her eyes. She had trusted him!

"James Foster?" she asked, stunned.

"You remember me. I'm flattered," Foster said.

"You were part of our crew, Foster! How can you do this?"

"Please," Foster said. "I was never part of your little crew. I've been working for The Monarchy for years. I was posing as your mechanic until the opportunity presented itself."

"What are you talking about?"

"I stayed on your ship until I knew we were heading to a major port. After a couple months in space, though, I was beginning to doubt we would ever go to a port city. I had to move things along myself. That cute little pilot of yours was going to save that transport ship. The core was cooling. I sent the passengers out and I rigged it so the core would melt down. It almost cost me. Thankfully, your brother got me out of there with only a knee injury and Shaw sent us to Port Frisco."

"We should've gone to King's Bay," Jordan said.

"That's the beauty of it," Foster said. "We had someone stationed at every port city. The Monarchy has people everywhere. Whichever port you eventually went to, I could contact that person and recommended them as my replacement."

"What's the problem, Foster? Did you not have the guts to do it yourself?"

"Everyone has skills, as I'm sure you're aware, Ms. Hawkins. I have enough engineering skills to pass as the ship's mechanic. However, when it came time to take you, we needed someone that could not only pilot the shuttle, but set the ground lock on your ship."

"I'm gonna kill both of you," Jordan said.

"Don't be so dramatic, Hawkins," Foster said. "A Monarchy scout ship is en route to pick you up and take you to our employer. I'm afraid this is the last time you'll see either one of us. Now, we need to get you out of this room and down to the warehouse floor. Your ride will be here soon."

* * *

Shaw, Brett, Jaimie, and Terry were dropped off by a small transport about three blocks from the shuttle. The streets here were littered with debris. It was like walking through a junkyard. Brett spotted the shuttle about one hundred feet from a large warehouse with several Monarchy markings on it.

"There's our shuttle," he said. "That warehouse looks like a good place to start looking. It's got Monarchy symbols all over it."

"Okay. Jaimie, you and Terry get the shuttle ready to go," Shaw said.

"Let's go, Terry," Jaime said.

Brett watched them make their way to the shuttle. He checked his handgun one more time. It was one of his favorite guns. It had never jammed or failed to fire. Still, didn't hurt to check it out. He also carried a backup pistol in the small of his back. He watched Shaw check his own weapon.

"Okay," Shaw said. "How are the communicators working?"

Brett heard Shaw's voice in his ear just fine, as well as the replies from Jaimie and Terry on the shuttle, and Donovan back at the ship. It was time to go into the warehouse, and Brett hoped they would find Jordan, unharmed.

* * *

Brett and Shaw entered the warehouse. There were only a few lights that seemed to work. Just inside the warehouse were stacks of boxes, barrels, and the gutted hulls of vehicles. Shaw led the way through the maze of junk. He signaled Brett to stop. Voices echoed in the warehouse. Brett recognized Jordan's. Good. They found her, and she was alive. He also made out two other voices. He and Shaw made their way further into the junk until they spotted an opening. Jordan was standing in the middle of the warehouse with her hands tied behind her back. On either side of her were Daniel Vesh and James Foster, the *Crash Wagon*'s previous two mechanics.

Shaw and Brett readied their weapons and slowly made their way toward Jordan. They stopped at the edge of the boxes, staying close to them in case they needed to take cover. They were about fifty feet away from Jordan and the two men guarding her. Shaw and Brett took aim at Foster.

"Foster!" Brett called.

Foster instinctively stepped behind Jordan to use her as a shield. Vesh turned around and saw the source of the voice. He was about two feet to the left of Jordan and Foster and he went for his holstered gun.

Brett quickly turned his gun on him. "Don't do it!" Do it, he thought.

Vesh stood motionless, looking his way. "How did you find us?"

"Shuttle has a tracker in it," Brett said.

"What about the ground lock?"

"We hired a mechanic that is much smarter than

you."

"The password?"

"The tattoo on your back."

"The doc. Should've known not to trust him," Vesh said. "You know. I may not be the smartest mechanic, as you've pointed out. But, I'm a very quick draw."

"You do see that I have my gun drawn and aimed at you already, don't you?" Brett asked.

"I do see that."

"And that's my sister you two have got tied up there. You know that, right?"

"That's right," Vesh said.

"Then you must also know that I will not hesitate to end you if you move."

"I don't think so, Hawkins. The way I heard it, if you hadn't hesitated nine years ago on New Year's Eve, the old man in Portozuela would be after you and not your sister." Vesh began walking toward Brett. "I think—"

The bullet from Brett's gun struck Vesh in the head. His lifeless body hit the ground. Brett then quickly aimed his weapon at Foster, the echo from the shot still ringing in the large warehouse. Foster pulled Jordan even closer to him.

"Well. You did tell him not to move," he said, looking at Vesh's body on the warehouse floor. He looked back at Shaw and Brett. Both had their guns aimed at him.

"Oh, what?" he asked. "You gonna open fire with me standing right behind her? I'm willing to bet neither one of you are that good."

"Just let her go, and we all walk out of here," Brett said.

"I don't think so, cowboy. In fact, there's a few more people that will be walking in here in just a minute. My employer is sending a scout ship to retrieve your sister."

"You know we can't let that happen," Shaw said.

"It's already happening, old man. You can't stop it."

Brett heard Jaimie's voice in his ear. "Guys. A small ship just landed behind the warehouse."

Brett and Shaw exchanged a glance.

"They're here, aren't they?" Foster asked.

"Let her go!" Brett said.

"Or what? You're in no position to negotiate."

The sound of a metal door sliding open at the back of the warehouse echoed through the dimly lit space. Foster smiled and glanced behind him to see three armed men entering the back of the warehouse through the large metal doors. It was the split-second Jordan needed.

She threw her head back, smashing it into Foster's nose, spun, and gave him a roundhouse kick to the left knee he had previously injured, dropping him to the floor. She dashed toward Brett and Shaw.

Foster got to his knees and drew his gun. The three men that entered the warehouse ran toward him.

"We want her alive!" one of the men yelled.

Foster fired his gun anyway, hitting Jordan in the leg before she could reach the cover Brett and Shaw hid behind.

The three men raised their guns and killed Foster before he could get another shot off. He fell, face forward, onto the concrete floor.

Brett and Shaw ran out and helped Jordan to her feet, supporting her between them as she hopped on one leg. They hurried back into the maze of boxes as the three men ran after them.

Brett knew that things weren't going exactly as planned, but they had Jordan. They just needed to get back to the shuttle. As long as they stayed close together and a good distance ahead, the men chasing them wouldn't fire. That was a little tougher with Jordan's injury.

"Split up," one of the men yelled.

Brett figured they would try to cut them off from the exit.

"Don't slow down!" he said. "We've got to keep moving!"

He saw the light of the exit at the front of the warehouse. The shuttle was maybe twenty or thirty yards away from the entrance. They were clearing the last bit of cover they had before heading out into the open. He paused to make sure the coast was clear.

"Okay, let's mo—"

The gun stock of one of the men swung around the corner and caught Brett in the face. He fell backwards and Jordan fell into Shaw, knocking him over. The man stood over Brett and raised his gun.

Well. I tried, Brett thought.

A loud clunk sounded and the man hit the floor. Behind him stood Terry Shannon. He was holding a piece of scrap metal.

"Jaimie was all like, 'Don't go!', and I was like, 'I can help!'" he said.

It was official. Brett owed Terry one. Two, if you counted isolating the ground lock.

Brett and Shaw helped Jordan back up. Brett handed Terry his backup pistol. "Cover our backs!"

"Let's move!" Shaw said.

Balancing Jordan between them, Brett and Shaw helped her to the shuttle. Terry was several yards behind them, looking to see if they were being chased. Brett heard gunfire and turned to see him firing wildly at the other two men that had stepped out of the warehouse. Terry was a terrible shot, but it forced the men to stop their pursuit and find cover just inside the door.

Brett and Shaw boarded the shuttle with Jordan. Brett looked back and saw Terry standing in the open, still unloading the pistol at the warehouse.

He drew his gun to cover him.

"Move, Shannon!"

Out of ammo, Terry turned to run to the shuttle, when a red mist sprayed from his right shoulder. He hit the ground, in obvious pain.

"Terry!" Jaimie yelled. She jumped out of the pilot's

seat and ran toward the open shuttle doors. Shaw grabbed her and pulled her to the floor as a hail of gunfire bounced off the hull.

"Your man can still be helped!" one of them yelled. "Let us have the girl, and we'll let you get him to a doctor. Or, we can finish him off right here. It's your choice."

Brett peeked around one of the open shuttle bay doors to assess the situation. The man that Terry knocked out had recovered and joined the other two. The first two men had their guns aimed at the shuttle, while the third had his aimed at Terry, waiting for the order to kill him.

"We don't have all day," the man said. "I'm guessing the girl is losing some blood. We wait around too long, and both of them bleed out. The way I see it, you give us the girl, alive, and you get your man, alive. Everyone wins."

* * *

Tears filled Jaimie's eyes as she watched Terry clutching his shoulder on the ground, maybe fifty feet away. She looked at Shaw, to the pilot's chair, then back at Shaw. "I have an idea!"

She ran back to the pilot's chair and spoke to Donovan through her communicator.

"Dr. Barrett?" Jaimie said.

"I've been listening, my dear. Tell me how to help."

"I need you to get to the bridge," Jaimie said. "Activate the RAID."

"On my way."

"You sure are taking your sweet time deciding what to do. The girl must not be in as bad of shape as I thought. Maybe this will speed up the process a little," the man yelled.

The man fired another shot at Terry, hitting him in the right leg. Terry screamed out in pain.

Shaw and Brett began firing a barrage of bullets in anger, hitting the cover the men were behind.

"Woo hoo!" one of the men yelled. "That stirred up a hornet's nest, didn't it, boys?"

Jaimie was shaking with adrenaline. "Doctor! Hurry!"

"Okay. I'm here. What do I do?"

"The RAID console is to the left of the main console. Activate it."

"Your man's situation seems to have gotten a little more dire," the man said. "You might want to seriously think about sending the girl over to us."

"Doctor?" Jaime asked.

"Done," Donovan said.

"Scan the area based on the coordinates I'm sending you now." She sent him the shuttle's current coordinates.

There was a short pause. "Done," Donovan said.

"You should see the shuttle readout on the screen."

"I see it."

"Keep scanning south until you see another small

ship." Jaimie tried to stay calm.

There was another pause. "Okay. I see it."

"Lock on to that ship, and transfer the control signal to the shuttle," Jaime said.

"Okay. You should have control, Ms. Ellis. Now what?"

"Now, we show them what stirring up a hornet's nest will do."

The sound of a ship was heard around the warehouse. Suddenly, the Monarchy scout ship turned the corner and hovered about thirty feet off the ground. It positioned itself between Terry and the men that were assaulting him. Two gatling guns rolled out of the side of the ship. The men ran into the warehouse.

"My turn," Jaimie said.

She engaged the gatling guns from the shuttle's console. They screamed to life, pouring round after round into the warehouse's entrance. As the front wall splintered, the men inside kept running.

"Whose situation is dire now?" she yelled.

Shaw and Brett dashed from the shuttle to get Terry. Jaimie could only imagine how loud it was there, and she hoped the spent shells weren't falling on them, but she had to keep firing. Once Shaw and Brett boarded with Terry, the captain turned to Jaimie.

"Get us out of here!"

Jaime sent the scout ship forward, crashing it into the warehouse entrance. It exploded in a flash of light and fire.

She then raised the shuttle into the sky, hit the thrusters, and sent it racing back to the *Crash Wagon*.

Chapter 7

Brett downed another shot of whiskey and set the glass back on the big wooden table in the galley. His jaw ached from the hit he took during Jordan's rescue. He rubbed it, hoping to dull the pain. The alcohol helped.

"You get the doc to look at that?" Shaw asked.

"No. I took a gun stock to the face. No cure for that. Just gonna be a little sore for a while."

"Maybe this will help a little," Shaw said, as he poured Brett another shot.

He downed it as Shaw poured one for himself.

"Doc says Terry's gonna be fine."

"Gotta admit. He showed some courage today," Brett said.

"He showed some stupidity."

"Same thing."

"I suppose," Shaw drank his shot. "You know what I find funny?"

"What's that?"

"I find it funny that out of all of us who came out of that warehouse, it was the old man who didn't get smacked in the face or shot."

"Don't worry, Captain. I'm sure there'll be plenty other opportunities for you to get smacked in the face or shot."

"There better not be," Shaw said, as he drank another shot. "I didn't get this ship and register with the Guild for that."

Brett poured himself another. "In all seriousness, Captain, I really am sorry that our past came down on the crew like this. It put everyone in danger. Got one of ours shot pretty bad."

"It all worked out. Terry will be fine."

"They're still out there. There's people out there that want revenge on Jordan. After today, they could be after all of us."

"Well," Shaw said. "We'll just have to be more careful. Look out for each other. That's what a crew does, right?"

"Right."

They each poured another shot and drank to the crew.

* * *

Donovan finished wrapping Jordan's leg.

"That should be fine. Just keep the bandage clean. I'll want to check on it at least once a day until further notice, so don't be a stranger."

"Thanks, Doc." Jordan stepped down off the exam table. Her leg hurt. She was gonna be sore for a few days. Terry? He was gonna hurt for a while.

Jordan and Donovan looked across the infirmary and saw Jaimie standing next to Terry's bed, speaking in low tones.

"What do you think about our new mechanic?" Jordan asked.

"He's leaps and bounds better than our last two, obviously. But I jest. In all seriousness, he is more than qualified from what I've heard. And, he displayed an unusual amount of courage, throwing himself in the line of fire to make sure you made it back to the shuttle safely."

"Why did he do that? He doesn't even know me."

"Count your blessings. If he knew you, he might not have done it."

"Nice."

"I thought you'd like that."

"Yeah, I'm not even mad."

* * *

Terry lay in bed, listening to Jaime tell him how concerned she was.

"I was terrified when they rushed you to the infirmary. I had just landed the shuttle in the ship. I couldn't get my seat harness off fast enough. Even when I finally got out of the shuttle, Captain sent me to the bridge to set a course for deep space. He didn't want to be around if The Monarchy sent another ship."

"Don't worry. I'm fine."

"Are you in any pain?"

"Not really. I've got some amazing medicine running through me right now. Doc fixed me up good. Just a little sore."

"You probably will be for a while."

"That was a pretty smart move you pulled. Transferring their ship controls to the shuttle."

"I use the RAID all the time on the *Crash Wagon*. First time I ever tried transferring control to the shuttle."

"That *was* a pretty good move, Ellis," Jordan said, as she walked over to Terry's bed. "I'm surprised you thought of it."

"Someone had to save you."

"I believe I played a small part in that," Donovan said.

"Yes, Doctor. We're all very proud." Jordan crossed her arms over her chest.

"Don't listen to her, Dr. Barrett. You were amazing," Jaimie said.

"Well, as amazing as I am, I'm going to have to ask

you two to wrap things up here. Mr. Shannon needs his sleep. If you'd like to join me in the galley, I'm late for drinks with the Captain and Mr. Hawkins."

"Thanks, Doc. We'll be there shortly," Jordan said.

Donovan left the infirmary and headed to the galley.

"Okay," Jaimie said to Terry. "Get some sleep." She leaned over and kissed him on the forehead. "You're my hero."

"Oh, god," Jordan said, rolling her eyes.

Jaimie turned to her. "And so are you!" She gave Jordan a big hug.

"Stop!" Jordan said.

Jaime let go, laughing at her reaction.

"You are so annoying."

"Whatever. You love me," Jaimie said. "I'm going to get some strawberries." She left the infirmary.

Jordan looked at Terry and shook her head. "No, she's not. I didn't get any when we restocked the galley."

"I'm sure she'll get over it. That is one cheerful girl."

"I think that's cause she eats too many strawberries."

Terry laughed. "Maybe that's it."

"Listen. I wanted to tell you that I appreciate what you did for me."

"Don't mention it."

"Okay. Well, get some sleep, like the doc says. I'm sure something on this ship is going to break soon. Either that, or we'll come across some poor travelers that need to get their ship running again."

"Okay," Terry said. "Have a drink for me."

"Will do." She left him alone in the infirmary.

Terry lay in bed, thinking about his new crew and how much he already liked it on this ship as he drifted off to sleep.

* * *

Jordan limped into the galley and sat at the table.

"Doc?" Shaw said. "Is Jordan on any type of medication that would prevent her from having a drink with us?"

"I hope not," Donovan said, before drinking his shot. "I'm currently on some of the same medication."

"Make it a double," Jordan said. "I'm drinking for Terry as well."

"That's awfully thoughtful of you," Brett said.

"What can I say? He really stuck his neck out for me."

"That's what a crew does," Brett said.

"No," Jordan said. "It's what a family does."

"If anyone needs to be treated for a toothache due to the sweetness of that comment, just let me know," Donovan said.

"Shut up," Jordan said.

"He's right, Jordan," Shaw said. "I can't think of anything sweeter."

"I can." Jaimie said, slamming the refrigerator door. She glared at Jordan. "Strawberries!"

Epilogue

Colin Flanagan walked the marble floor, each step echoing down the corridor leading to Mr. Capizzi's office. The job had been a failure and someone was going to pay for that. He had given bad news to Mr. Capizzi on many prior occasions. Sometimes the old man dealt with it calmly, sometimes not. Being the head of The Monarchy crime family meant getting bad news from time to time. He wondered how he would react to finding out the woman that killed his son was still out there.

Flanagan entered the office and saw Mr. Capizzi sitting at his desk. A large window wrapped the wall behind him, giving a wide view of the Portozuela streets below.

"What is it?" Capizzi asked.

"I've got some bad news," Flanagan said.

"Jordan Hawkins?"

"They didn't get her."

Mr. Capizzi stood up from his desk. He turned and looked through the window, across the vast city.

"Losses?" Capizzi asked.

"Both contacts, the ship, and the warehouse in Port of Orleans. The lads you sent to pick her up are on a transport head'n back. They're treat'n some injuries."

"Still think my fee is too high?" a woman's voice asked.

Flanagan turned and drew his gun in the same motion. The woman was very tall, very beautiful, and very armed. She also had a laser sight from Flanagan's gun marking its target right between her eyes.

"Stand down, Flanagan," Capizzi said. "I invited her here."

Flanagan lowered his gun, but kept a suspicious eye on the woman. "Who is she?"

"Elizabeth Porter," the woman said. "You don't have to talk as if I'm not standing right here."

Flanagan holstered his gun. "You're Porter? I've heard about you. You were once Captain Porter if my recollection serves me. You led a group of pirates. That is, until there was a mutiny. How many of your own lads did you kill that day? The numbers are a tad fuzzy."

"An interesting question, coming from someone that's killed more people than the Red Flu," Porter said.

"You think you know me, lass?"

"I know you're from Strathmore."

"Figure that one out on your own, did you? My accent didn't have anything to do with that, now did it?"

"Enough," Mr. Capizzi said. "You two will have plenty of time to get to know each other even better."

Flanagan didn't like the sound of that. "If you don't mind me asking, sir. What do you mean?"

"Ms. Porter's your new partner."

Guess Capizzi wasn't the only one to get bad news today.

From The Author

Thanks for reading the first book in the *Crash Wagon* series! I hope you had fun reading it. You can find other books by me here:

www.amazon.com/author/JasonEricPryor

The best way to find out about my future releases is to sign up on my mailing list. You will NOT be spammed. You will only receive email from me regarding book releases, special promotions, and other book related news.

www.JasonEricPryor.com

Questions or comments? Email me at JasonEricPryor@gmail.com

One other thing...

If you enjoyed reading my book, please take a minute to leave a review. It doesn't have to be long or wordy if you don't want it to be. Just a brief comment on what you thought of the book will be quick and painless, and I'll be eternally grateful.

Book Two Excerpt

I hope you've enjoyed reading *Crash Wagon: Book One - Family Ties*. As an added bonus, I'm including an excerpt here from *Crash Wagon: Book Two*. As of this writing, I'm still working on the second book. What you're about to read has not been edited, and may not even be in the final version of the book once it's completed. It's raw. I just thought it might be fun to include it for you guys. Enjoy!

*** Excerpt from *Crash Wagon: Book Two* ***

"Is he dying?" Jordan asked. She sat at the table, drinking a cup of coffee while Shaw stood at the stove, cooking eggs and bacon.

"I doubt it. He just said he was going for a walk," Shaw said.

"He just said he was going for a walk?"

"That's what he said. I mean, Terry likes to start working early, so I get that."

"And, Jaimie likes to be where Terry is, so I get that. But, the doc?"

"Yeah. It confuses me too. Especially since he hates this place so much. But, I wasn't going to question him. He needs to get out more. It's good for him."

"Can't argue with that," Jordan said.

Brett walked into the galley and stretched.

"What's good for who?" he asked. "Oh, and I don't know what you two are talking about, but I'm sure that, whatever it is, You could definitely argue with it." he said to Jordan.

"I'm gonna have to side with your brother on that one."

"I shouldn't have to take this from you two. I haven't even finished my coffee yet," Jordan said.

"Them's the breaks, kid," Brett said as he poured himself a cup of coffee. "Why are you cooking breakfast, Captain?"

"Well, it's morning. Breakfast is the meal that's traditionally eaten in the morning. I just put two and two together and this is what I came up with."

Jordan smiled at Shaw's comment and took another drink of her coffee.

"No, I mean, we could've probably just walked to Hotel Dixon over there. Based on the spread he put out last night, he's probably got a buffet over there right now, money not being an issue and all," Brett said.

"You're probably right. But, I think I'd rather stay right here on the ship and eat. We go over there, he'd say something about Jordan's place again, she'd shoot him, and all we'd have for payment is a piece of ice in a plastic cube and the titanium base it sits on."

"I'd like to kick him in his place," Jordan said.

Shaw scooped some eggs and bacon on to a couple of plates and set them down in front of Brett and Jordan.

"I'm thinking, the sooner we get this job done and get out of here, the better."

"I say we forget the job and leave now," Brett said. "We don't need the money *that* bad."

"It's a contract job, Brett," Shaw said as he fixed himself a plate. "Normally, we can decide whether a job is worth our while. You accept a contract from the Guild, you do the job or run the risk of losing your license. With the exception of Dixon being a huge chore, the job is an easy payday."

"I guess," Brett said. "I just can't wait to get it done and get out of here."

"Good thing Terry got an early start then," Jordan said.

"He's already out there?"

"Yeah. Jaimie took him some coffee and, get this, the doc is out there too."

"The doc? Is he dying?"

*** End of excerpt ***

About The Author

Hey guys and gals! I'm Jason.

I thought I would tell you a little bit more about me. So, here goes.

I've always had a love for storytelling. Books, movies, TV, comics, art, music, poetry, cave paintings, smoke signals, whatever. If it tells a good story, I'm interested.

I'm an amateur photographer. I have a degree in professional photography from the New York Institute of Photography, but I don't really consider myself a professional photographer since I've only had a few paying gigs. I'm a huge fan of all different types of photos.

I love music and I enjoy playing the guitar. Being raised in the Mississippi Delta, (in a small town called Greenwood, Mississippi), I'm naturally a big fan of the blues. I've lived most of my life between Memphis, Tennessee and New Orleans, Louisiana, so I have a very rich musical heritage. I enjoy music of all kinds, but I'll pay extra attention to it if there's a nice guitar playing.

I have many other interests including art (I love pencil sketching and digital painting), architecture (I worked at an architecture firm for 5 years), and fitness (I have a gym membership...and I use it). I also train with a personal trainer that is a great motivator and friend.

I currently live on the Gulf Coast in a town called

Mobile, Alabama. This is where I write books, draw pictures, play music, workout with my trainer, and plot world domination. (Don't worry. I will be a kind and understanding overlord.)

If you would like to keep up with what's going on with me and my writing, you can do that at several places.

My official site is:
www.JasonEricPryor.com
(Add your email to my mailing list to receive an email whenever I release a new book or have a special promotion. You will only receive email from me regarding book releases, special promotions, and other book related news.)

"Like" my Facebook page at:
www.facebook.com/JasonEricPryor

Follow me on Twitter at:
twitter.com/JasonEricPryor

Acknowledgements

Many people, through their support, encouragement, and skills, have helped make this book a reality. I want to thank them all from the bottom of my heart.

I would like to thank my great editor and teacher, Jennifer Feddersen. Not only did you teach me a lot about writing, you helped me gain confidence in my ability to write. Working with you is a joy!

I would also like to thank my amazingly talented cover artist, Tom Edwards. One of the most exciting parts of creating this book was receiving the cover artwork in my email at various stages of design. You never failed to impress. It is so much fun working with you!

I want to thank the guys and gals, past and present, that write on the Oberon and Salvation cooperative writing forum. To be around people that not only share my love of writing, but my love of a certain 'Verse, is an amazing experience. You are all so talented, each and every one, and you teach me so much. Keep flyin' my friends!

I want to say 'thank you' to all my family and friends that have supported me as I wrote this book. More importantly, they have supported me throughout my life.

I write to entertain myself and others, and to provide a temporary escape from normal life. But, it's always nice to come back to that normal life because that's where the people I love are.

Finally, I want to thank you, the reader. I want to thank you for giving me a chance to entertain you for a little while. I sincerely hope you have enjoyed this book and will enjoy future releases from me.

Thank you all!